A BABY FOR THE NAVY SEAL

BE MY BABY

SHAW HART

*

I've always wanted him. Just not like this…

I've been in love with my brother's best friend since we were kids.

Anson is the only man that I've ever wanted.

Too bad for me, he only seems to see me as his best friend's little sister.

I thought that when he left for the military, things would get easier.

That maybe my feelings would fade, maybe I could forget him when he's away on deployments.

I should have known better.

Until, one drunken night, it seems that maybe he sees me as more than a little sister to him after all.

When I wake up the next morning, he's gone, and I try to hold onto the memory of our one night together.

Except I have more than the memory because it seems that Anson has left me a little keepsake of our one night together.

And in nine months, I'll have a surprise for my sexy Navy SEAL as well.

ONE

Lottie

I'M STARTING to wonder why I still live in Los Angeles. I dread leaving my apartment to go get groceries since I know it will take me an hour in this traffic to get anywhere.

"I should just move already," I mumble to myself as I dig through my dresser to try to find a clean shirt.

I keep telling myself that I should find a new city, somewhere cheaper. I think that maybe it's time that I get a change of scenery or maybe an apartment that didn't cost an arm and leg, but I know that I won't. I could never leave when my family is here.

I live here with my brother, Rhett, and his best friend, Anson. They're the only bit of family that I have left, and I would hate to be away from them. It's more than that though.

I've been in love with my brother's best friend since I was just a kid. He was like a knight in shining armor, riding in and rescuing me from my awful parents. Well, maybe not rescuing since he was just a kid himself, but he did his best to protect me.

My brother did too and the three of us grew close, bonding over our terrible parents and childhoods. The more time I spent around Anson, the more I fell for him. He was so charming, even when we were kids, and so patient with me. There were times when Rhett wanted to watch TV or ride his bike, but Anson would stay and play dolls with me. He's the one who bought me my first art pad and who encouraged me to start my own business.

I fell more and more in love with him with each passing day. Now, it's been years and he's ruined me for any other man.

Too bad for me, he only seems to see me as his best friend's little sister and not the love of his life.

I sigh as I slip the shirt over my head and pad barefoot out of my room and over to the kitchen. My coffee is probably ice cold by now but I barely slept last night and I need all of the caffeine that I can get.

I wince as I swallow a mouthful and grab my phone. I pull up my to do list, ignoring the big bold sentence at the top of the list. I need to go get groceries, finish up my latest client's project, and pick up the apartment a little bit.

My eyes stray to the thing at the top of the list and my heart kicks against my ribs as I read the words.

ANSON COMES HOME!!!

My heart is racing and I swallow hard as nerves hit me. Both my brother and Anson are in the Navy. They're SEALs to be exact and they tend to get deployed pretty regularly. This is one of the only times they have been deployed together. They were split into separate teams for this last deployment and now Anson is coming home and my brother just left a few weeks ago to start his.

I'm both excited and nervous to be alone with Anson for so long. I know that he'll have to do training and meetings on the base, but he'll have some time off. We'll be alone in this apartment every night, and I'm not sure that I'll be able to hold myself back from confessing to him that I love him.

It will be nice not to be in this apartment all alone anymore. I try to focus on that and not that I'll be alone with Anson as I pick up the kitchen and wipe down the counters. I'm not sure when Anson will get here but I'd like to have all of my errands done before he gets home.

My phone rings and I jump to answer it, wondering if it's Anson. It's not. Instead, it's my best friend, Goldie.

"Hey, aren't you at work?" I ask, and she sighs.

"Yeah, but I'm not doing anything. Boss Man is in a meeting so I'm just sitting here. Bored out of my mind."

"And so, you thought of me," I joke, and she laughs.

"I did. I'm glad that you get it," she says. "So, today is the big day…"

"Yep."

There's a moment of silence where Goldie waits for me to start to ramble about Anson coming home. She's been listening to me gush about him for the last fifteen years, and she's all for me telling him how I feel. She doesn't get that me telling him could ruin everything between us.

"He's coming home today. I still need to go get groceries and clean up a bit, but he could be home at any time," I start, and I know without her saying anything that she's smiling.

"Why don't you just tell him that you love him already?" She suggests for the millionth time.

"Because when he rejects me, it will ruin everything," I remind her, and she sighs.

"Okay, then don't say anything. Just walk around the

apartment naked. When he gets home, just be like, 'oh my gosh! I forgot that you were coming back today! This is so embarrassing,' but like let him get a good look, and then he'll just ravish you," she says.

"Who is ravishing who?" Goldie's boss asks.

"How was the meeting?" She counters, and I'm sure that he's glaring at her.

Goldie's boss, or Boss Man, as she calls him, is always trying to get Goldie to open up. I think he's in love with her, but Goldie doesn't see it that way. She wants to keep her personal and professional life private, which seems to drive him crazy.

"Is that a personal call?" he asks.

"Nope," she lies.

"You talk about people ravishing other people with our clients?" he asks drily.

"Yep. Why do you think business has been so good since I got here?"

I laugh, and she clears her throat.

"Anyway, go get him, girl," she says, and I laugh.

"I'll talk to you later," I promise.

"Good. Love you!"

"Hey!" Boss Man shouts, and she hangs up before I can hear what else he's going to say about her telling someone that she loves them.

I chuckle, tucking my phone back into my pocket before I grab my purse. *I'll go to the grocery store first and then clean,* I decide.

I'm slipping my shoes on when there's a knock at the door, and I frown. It's probably a delivery man, though I didn't order anything recently.

Maybe Rhett sent me a package.

I pull open the door, and my mouth drops open when I

see Anson standing there with a wide grin on his handsome face. His dark brown hair is still short, cut into the typical military haircut. He seems bigger than the last time I saw him, and I wonder how much he was working out on this last deployment.

"Lottie!" He shouts, his green eyes sparkling as he opens his arms wide for a hug, and I grin, launching myself at him.

He catches me easily, wrapping his strong arms around me as he lifts me off my feet. My heart is racing out of control, and I can feel a blush staining my cheeks as I bury my face in his neck and cling to him.

"It's so good to see you," he says, and I nod, still holding onto him.

"Welcome home, Anson," I whisper, and his grip on me tightens.

TWO

Anson

IT FEELS SO right to have her in my arms.

It always has. That was one of the first clues that I was in love with my best friend's little sister.

I don't want to let her go, but I know that she'll probably think it's strange if I just keep crushing her against me like this. Feeling her curves pressed against me is starting to have an effect on my body so I let her slide down to her feet, clearing my throat and praying that she doesn't notice my erection bulging the front of my jeans.

I'm jet lagged like hell, but I think I could be half dead and I would still get a hard-on if Lottie was anywhere in the vicinity.

She's had that effect on me since we were just teenagers, though I think I was in love with her before I even knew what love was. I've always loved being around Lottie. I wanted to keep her safe. I wanted to make her happy.

We both got the short end of the stick in the parent department. Mine were abusive, but Lottie's were just plain neglectful. They'd leave for weeks at a time, rarely stocked the refrigerator, and there was that one month where they never paid the heating bill. We spent that month huddling under all the blankets in the house together.

I used to spend all of my free time at their house. They only lived a few doors down, and their house, while void of food and heat, was still favorable to getting smacked around at mine.

Rhett quickly became my best friend, and together we did everything we could to protect Lottie from our parents and the evils of the world. It's also my friendship with Rhett that has stopped me from claiming Lottie.

I would never do anything to hurt Rhett or my friendship with him. He means too much to me. They both do, and I don't want to ruin that by trying to date Lottie. The two of them have become my family, and I don't want to lose either one of them.

Besides, Lottie deserves a hell of a lot better than me. She deserves a hell of a lot better than the life of a Navy SEAL wife.

"I didn't know that you would be back so soon," Lottie says as she takes a step back from me.

"Yeah, I landed at like seven and then had to in process, but I'm done for the day, and I have the next three days off. Were you headed out?" I ask when I notice that she's wearing shoes.

"Yeah, I need to go to the grocery store."

"I'll go with you," I tell her, and she nods.

I'm exhausted, and I probably should go inside and take a shower and then get some sleep, but I never could resist spending time with Lottie.

"Let me just put my bags inside."

She nods, and I head inside and into my room. It smells like Lottie. The whole apartment does, and I love it. She smells like oranges and cinnamon.

It's good to be home, but that doesn't stop me from worrying about Rhett being over there without me having his back. My last deployment got a little dicey a few times, and I'm concerned for my friend. I know that Rhett can handle himself, but that still doesn't stop me from worrying about him.

I got to see him a little bit when he arrived a few days ago, and it was good to hang out with him. He made me promise to look after Lottie while he was gone, and of course, I told him that I would.

I just wish that I could look after all of her needs...

Lottie's phone dings as I come back into the living room, and she curses as she reads the message.

"Is everything okay?" I ask her, and she nods distractedly.

"My client needs the work done today before closing. Do you think we could run to the store in like an hour or so? That way I can finish it now."

"Of course. I'll go take a shower while you work. Let me know when you're ready to go."

She nods, giving me a bright smile as she heads into her room. I watch her go before I turn back to my own room and head for the bathroom.

I roll out my shoulders as I peel off my shirt and toss it into the hamper. I turn the water on in the shower before I unbutton my pants and strip out of the last of my clothes.

I groan as I step beneath the hot spray. It feels good to take a shower with some privacy and with full water pressure.

I reach for my body wash, and my eyes snag on a brightly colored bottle. It's Lottie's body wash, and I wonder how it got in my shower.

Maybe hers was acting up?

My hand pauses as I reach for mine, and I find myself grabbing hers instead. I love her scent, and I can't resist having it all over my body. I squirt some into my hand, and my cock gets hard at the scent of her.

"Fuck," I hiss as I reach down and wrap my fist around my thick length.

I give myself a few pumps, trying to take the edge off, but I can't seem to stop there. I haven't seen her in months, and it's all too much. I need her, but I can't have her so this will have to do.

I start to envision her giving me one of those sly grins, her pale blue eyes twinkling as she beams at me. Her black hair is longer, and I wonder if it's long enough that I could wrap it around my hand. I could use it like that to tug her hand back and kiss her while I fuck her from behind.

My dick swells in my hand as I picture her in a million different positions. Lottie on her knees in front of me, my dick stretching her lips as she takes more and more of me down her throat. Or maybe up against the wall that separates our bedrooms. Does she like it rough and fast or soft and slow?

I wonder if she tastes like oranges and cinnamon too. I could spread her thick thighs and find out. How many orgasms could I lick her to? Would she like to come all over my face?

I've been dying to know the answer to those questions since I was fifteen. It's starting to kill me that I still don't know.

I'm full-on jerking off, and a part of me hates myself for

not being able to control myself. It's just been too long, and now I'm surrounded by her scent. This is the better alternative to fucking her in real life.

My dick jerks in my hands as I think about her curves pressed against me. I imagine her tongue teasing my cock before she opens her mouth wide and sucks me into her sweet mouth.

"That's it, baby. Take it all," I encourage her.

She moans, eager to do as I ask.

"Good girl," I praise her. *"Now swallow around my cock."*

She buries my length in her throat, swallowing around me, and I groan, my eyes rolling back in my head as she does it again.

"Such a good fucking girl," I moan, and she grins up at me. *"Now I need that pussy of yours. Is it wet for me?"*

"Uh-huh," she says, giving me a sly smirk.

I reach down, lifting her up into my arms, and she goes willingly, wrapping her legs around my waist as I press her back against the shower wall.

My cock finds her snug hole, and we both cry out as I thrust inside her snug hole.

"Fuck, baby. Did you miss me?" I ask, and she nods.

"So much. So, so much," she moans as I start to pound into her.*

I can feel my orgasm starting to build inside of me, and I know that I won't be able to hold off for much longer.

"Come inside me. I want to feel it, Anson," she purrs, and I grit my teeth.

"You want my come, baby?" I ask her, and she nods as I bounce her on my cock.*

Her big tits are bouncing in my face, and I wish that I

had laid her down so that I could suck on her nipples while I fuck her.

"Then beg me," I order her.

"Please, Anson. I need it. Come inside of me. Fill me up. I want to feel your come dripping out of me all day."

With those sultry words whispered in my ear, I can't hold back any longer, and I give us what we both want, coming deep inside of her.

I come all over the shower wall and my hands, and I blink my eyes open, the daydream of Lottie and me disappearing.

My heart drops, and my whole body sags as the orgasm fades, and I'm left feeling cold and alone.

This is bad.

This is really bad.

I'm getting more and more obsessed with my girl.

I wonder when I'm finally going to snap.

THREE

Lottie

"ARE you sure that you don't want me to grab one of those?" I ask Anson as we carry the groceries up the stairs to our apartment.

He has about ten bags in his hands, while I only have two. I tried to take more from the trunk, but he wouldn't let me. Still, I feel bad watching him carry everything.

"I've got it. You just get the door," he says, and I roll my eyes as I jog up the stairs, digging my keys out of my purse.

I let us in, and Anson dumps the groceries onto the kitchen counter. I catch him yawning and smile. I knew he was tired, but it's nice that he still went with me to run errands.

"Why don't you go take a nap or something while I make us dinner?"

"I can help you cook," he offers, but he smothers another yawn when he says that.

"I've got it. I wanted to do this for you anyway. Don't ruin it for me."

"I would never," he says, holding up his hands as he backs out of the room.

I watch him head down the short hallway and disappear into his room before I get started on putting everything away. I leave the ingredients for dinner out and put some music on my phone before I get started cooking.

Goldie texts me as I'm sliding the chicken into the oven, and I smile when I see her message.

GOLDIE: Is he home yet? Were you naked?

Goldie: Did you finally tell him that you love him??

I SMILE as I text her back, knowing she'll be disappointed in my answers.

LOTTIE: Yes, no, and no.

Goldie: Bummer.

Goldie: It's not too late! Strip!!

Lottie: Absolutely not.

Goldie: You're going to die alone.

Lottie: That's not true. I'll have you.

Goldie: And all of our cats.

I PUT my phone away and get started on the potatoes while the chicken cooks. I can't help but wonder if maybe Goldie is right. What's my plan here? To die alone? To wait until

Anson finally settles down and then try to find someone that I would probably only love half as much?

Either way, things are going to end in heartbreak.

I sigh, grabbing the bottle of wine we bought and opening it. I pour myself a glass and then grab another when I see Anson come out of his bedroom.

"Wine?" I ask, holding up the bottle, and he nods.

"Is dinner already done?"

"No, it will be about another twenty minutes or so."

He nods, taking a healthy swallow from his glass.

"How was your deployment?" I ask him, and he pauses.

I can tell then that it wasn't one of the easy deployments.

"It was fine. I missed Rhett, but I'm sure you were glad to have him here."

"He said that he saw you the last few days," I comment and he nods.

"Yeah, we got to room next to each other for a few days while I was out processing. How's your job going here?" he asks.

"Good! I've gotten a few new clients, and almost everyone has been back for more orders. My schedule is actually about as full as I can get."

"That's awesome, Lottie! I knew that you would be a success," he says with a proud smile.

The timer for the potatoes goes off, and I move to pull them out of the oven.

"Want me to set the table?" Anson offers, and I nod.

"Sure."

I put the potatoes into a bowl and then grab the chicken out of the oven and the green beans from off the stove.

"Everything looks great," Anson compliments me, and I smile.

"Hopefully it tastes great too!"

Anson refills our wine glasses, and we both start to fill our plates with food. We talk and joke over dinner, getting caught up on everything that's happened over the last few months. The wine is flowing, and before I know it, we've finished one bottle and opened another.

"Want to sit in the living room?" Anson asks, and I nod, feeling a little lightheaded as I stand to follow him.

Anson grabs the remote, putting on a movie I've never seen before. I try to pay attention to the plot, but the wine is starting to make everything fuzzy.

I take another sip and find myself moving closer to him on the couch. Anson lifts his arm, wrapping it around my shoulders as I snuggle into his side.

"You're so warm," I sigh, and he chuckles.

"Are you cold?"

"Not anymore," I say as I wrap my arm around his middle.

We've never really cuddled like this before. It seemed too dangerous before, and I'm struggling to remember why right now. It feels so right.

I bury my face in his neck, breathing in his scent. He kind of smells like me, and I giggle at the thought.

"What's so funny?" Anson asks, his voice low and slightly slurred.

I can't tell if he's actually slurring, though, or if it's just in my head.

"You smell like me," I tell him, laughing harder now.

I can't remember why that was so funny, and I giggle as I try to figure it out. I pull back slightly to see if Anson thinks it's as funny as I do, and my laughter cuts off when I realize how close we are.

My breasts are pressed up against his side, and his arm

is wrapped around my shoulders, keeping me in place. Our thighs are touching, and there's something so intimate in the contact.

His warm breath fans over my face, and my eyes drop to his lips. They look so warm and inviting, and I find myself swaying closer to him.

"Lottie," he whispers, and I nod.

I'm not sure who moves closer to the other first, but I suppose it doesn't matter. Anson's lips are on mine, and I wrap my arms around his neck, crushing our chests together. My nipples are standing at attention, eager for the contact with Anson's strong chest.

"So damn sweet," he murmurs against my mouth, and his words send a rush of lightning straight to my core.

I need more.

We're wrapped around each other, and I love it. I've never felt anything better in my entire life. I've never felt anything more right in my life. I was meant to be in Anson's arms.

His kiss tastes like longing with a tinge of desperation, and I wonder if maybe, possibly, he's wanted this for just as long as I have.

He nips at my bottom lip, and I gasp, giving him the opening he was looking for. His tongue swipes against my bottom lip before it slips inside to tangle with mine, and I moan, my nails digging into his shoulders as I hold on for dear life.

He shifts on the couch, lifting me up easily, and I gasp in shock as I'm placed in his lap. I part my legs reflexively, my knees landing on the couch cushions on either side of him.

"That's better," he murmurs, his green eyes dark with need.

As I settle over his hard length, I have to agree.

This is so much better.

My hands find their way into his hair, and I tug him closer, needing his mouth back on mine. He comes willingly, taking over as soon as our lips touch. He deepens the kiss almost immediately, and I sigh, sinking back into him.

My head is swimming, but it's not from the wine. This is all Anson.

His hands cup my ass, and I wiggle against him, both of us groaning when I drag my center over his stiff cock.

"More," I breathe against his lips, and then the world shifts beneath me as Anson lifts us, turning me and then laying me down on the couch.

He gives me a cocky grin as he comes down over me, and I just smile as his lips find mine once more.

FOUR

Anson

SHE'S SO RESPONSIVE.

Every swipe of my tongue or press of my body against hers earns me one of those breathy moans that's starting to drive me out of my mind.

Every flick of her tongue or brush of her fingers against my skin only spurs me on more, and I find myself snaking my hand up her shirt and cupping her breast.

"So perfect," I say more to myself than her.

She arches her back, offering more of herself to me, and somewhere in my brain, warning bells are going off, but I'm too far gone to think about the consequences of all of this right now. I've wanted this girl for so long, and now that she's beneath me, I can't stop. Not unless she asks me to.

I squeeze her tits in my hands, making her moan. Her nipples harden to diamond points against my palms, and I know I need to see them. I need to feel them in my mouth.

"Been imagining these for so long," I tell her, trailing kisses down her neck as I tug her shirt up.

She lifts up, helping me pull it off, and then I reach for her bra and toss that aside too. My mouth waters at the sight that greets me.

Her tits are even better than I had imagined, and I groan as I cup them in my hands, pinching her hard nipples. She gasps, arching against my touch, and I lean down, capturing one of the stiff peaks in my mouth and sucking.

"Anson!" She cries out, and I grin against her flesh.

I love hearing her say my name like that.

Her legs are restless around my hips, and I wonder if her panties are soaked for me.

"Are you wet for me, baby?" I ask her, switching between her tits.

She nods, her eyes half-lidded as she stares up at me. She's never looked sexier.

"I can't wait to see these big titties bouncing when I fuck you."

"Please," she begs, and I lick her nipple.

"Please what, baby? What do you need?"

"You!" She shouts, and I grin.

I kiss her between her breasts and then start to sink down her body. A part of my brain urges me to move us to the bedroom, but it's too far away. I need Lottie now.

My hands grip her pants, tugging them and her panties down her legs.

"So wet, baby. Is this all for me?" I ask, my thumb swiping up her drenched center.

"Yes, yes, yes," she chants, her eyes sliding closed at my touch.

"Watch me while I lick this sweet pussy," I say, pinching her clit slightly, and her eyes snap open.

Her pale blue eyes meet mine, and I try to imprint this memory in my brain. Lottie, sprawled on the couch, her body flushed with arousal, her tits wet from my mouth. My cock protests still being in my jeans, but I ignore him, dipping my head and getting my first taste of my girl.

She's so sweet and perfect. I can't get enough. I push my hands against her curvy thighs, spreading her wider, and she cries out as I spear my tongue into her snug hole.

"Anson!" She cries, and I do it again.

I've never been with anyone before. A couple of the guys in basic training and BUDS tried to set me up, but I never wanted anyone but Lottie.

She's so snug, and my heart leaps as I wonder if maybe she was saving herself for me too.

"Are you a virgin, baby?" I ask, needing to know.

She nods, her cheeks stained with a pretty blush.

"I've never... I've never wanted anyone," she says, and I nod.

"Good girl."

Then my face is buried back in her sticky sweet pussy, and I eat her like a man starved. My cock swells even further in my pants as her hands grip the short strands of my hair, and she holds me to her. As if I would try to get away.

"Anson, please. I need more," she begs, and I nod.

I slowly work one finger into her as I find her clit and suck it into my mouth. She almost shoots off the couch, and I use my other hand, gripping her hip and holding her in place. She's calling my name, screaming it over and over again, and I let the sound become a symphony in my head as I work another finger into her.

She's so tight, and I don't want to hurt her, but if the sounds she's making are any indication, she's not in any pain.

I work my fingers in and out of her, my tongue rolling in tight circles over her clit until her legs tense on either side of my head. She seems to hold her breath, and I glance up her body as her face tips back to the ceiling. Then she's coming all over my face, and I grit my teeth to keep from coming in my jeans.

"Oh," she sighs, coming back down to Earth, and I hurry to strip off my clothes as she blinks her eyes open at me.

"Your turn," she purrs, and I shake my head.

"I need you," I tell her, gripping my cock, and she glances down at the straining monster that can't wait to be inside her for another second.

Precum is dripping from the head, and she licks her lips.

"Fuck," I hiss, pinching the tip of my dick. "I need you, baby."

She nods, spreading her legs wider, and I fall on her, kissing her lips as I guide my cock to her entrance.

We both tense as I start to work the head of my dick into her, and I kiss her, trying to distract her from the pain that I know she's going to feel when I pop her cherry.

I want to tell her that I love her, that I've always loved her, but the words get caught in my throat, strangled by a moan as I feel her silky walls contract around the tip of my dick.

"Fuck," I hiss out, and she nods.

"More."

I work another inch into her, bumping up against her virginity, and I grit my teeth. She's looking up at me with so much trust in her blue eyes, and I hate the thought of hurting her.

"I want you," she tells me, and I nod, taking a deep

breath before I thrust fully into her, breaking her cherry and giving us what we both need.

She cries out, her pussy clenching around my length, and I kiss her, trying to do whatever I can to ease the pain.

When her lips start to soften under mine, I know that she's okay, and I pull back slightly before I sink inside her. We pick up a steady rhythm, and soon our bodies are moving together in perfect harmony.

"You feel so good," she moans as I trail kisses down her neck.

My lips wrap around one stiff nipple, and I suck it into my mouth as I start to fuck her harder. I can feel her tightening around me, knowing we're both so close.

She wraps her legs around my waist, and I fuck her deeper.

"Anson," she gasps, and I angle my hips, making sure to hit that same spot over and over again.

She tightens around me further, and her breath catches in her lungs. Her orgasm slams into her almost violently, like an earthquake beneath her skin, and her release triggers my own.

She screams my name, her voice sounding hoarse, and the caveman in me loves that I did that to her.

I come with her, my release seeming to go on for minutes, and then we're both panting, our bodies coated in a light sheen of sweat as we cling to each other. Her face is buried in my neck, and I pull out, shifting us on the couch so that her back is pressed against the back of the couch and I'm at her front.

"That was," I murmur, and she sighs.

I look down, noticing that her eyes are closed, her breathing evening out, and I know she's asleep.

I smile down at her.

I must have really worn her out.

I gather her up in my arms, replaying what happened again in my brain as I let my eyes drift shut.

We can wake up like this tomorrow.

Tomorrow.

My eyes snap open, and I tense as my heart starts to race out of control.

Oh my god, what have I done?

I know what I've done. Me fucking Lottie on our couch is playing on a loop inside my head as she dozes in my arms.

Did I just ruin my relationship with everyone who means the most to me? Rhett will kill me if he finds out I slept with his little sister. Not only slept with her but popped her cherry.

How could I do this to him?

How could I do this to her?

Did I just fuck everything up between us because I couldn't keep my dick in my pants?

I've been holding myself back, denying my feelings for her since I was fifteen years old, and as soon as Rhett is gone, I slip up. I should have known that this would happen. Getting drunk when the two of us were all alone was a mistake.

Oh my fucking god. What if she was drunk and didn't know what she was doing? I mean, I thought we were both a little tipsy but not anywhere close to drunk.

What if she regrets it? What if she never wanted me in that way?

And I just took her virginity.

I wince, dragging my hand down my face.

How did I manage to screw everything up so fast?

Everyone will leave you. You'll drive them all away.

That's what my old man told me the day I moved out. I hadn't wanted to believe him, but maybe he's right.

I'm such an asshole. I betrayed my best friend, and I know that I probably made everything awkward between Lottie and me.

I know this will hurt her, but I can't stay here any longer. Self-disgust is overtaking me, and I can't think straight. I need to get out of here and clear my head. Then I can come up with a plan on how to fix this.

I move slowly, shifting Lottie further back onto the couch and tucking the blanket around her. I get dressed as quietly as I can and take one last look at Lottie before I grab my keys and head out.

I jog down the stairs to my car and slip behind the wheel.

Then I freeze.

Where am I supposed to go now? I have a few friends at the base that I could crash with for a few days, but it's late, almost two in the morning and I hate to wake them up.

I reach for my phone, scrolling until I find his number and hit dial.

"What?" Theo snaps as soon as the call connects, and I bite back a grin.

"Good morning to you too, sunshine," I joke, and he huffs out a sigh.

"Are you back in the states then?" He asks.

"Yeah. I got back yesterday."

"We'll have to do dinner."

"How about an early breakfast instead?" I suggest, and I hear his chair creak.

Theo is a lawyer and a complete workaholic. He was a grade ahead of Rhett and me in high school, and after he graduated, he went to Harvard and then law school while

Rhett and I enlisted. We've stayed in touch, though, and now that we're stationed in Los Angeles, close to his law office, we try to meet up at least once a month.

"The diner? In twenty?" He asks, and I smile.

"See you soon."

I hang up, starting my car, but I pause before I can shift into drive. It feels wrong to leave Lottie. I can't help but think that she's going to be hurt if she wakes up alone, but I can't seem to get myself to go back upstairs. Not right now, anyway. I need to see Theo. I need to talk about this with someone. Then I'll have a plan and know how to handle all of this.

I look in the rearview mirror one last time before I shift and take off down the mostly deserted streets toward downtown.

I reach the diner at the same time as Theo, and he nods as he heads my way.

"Good to see you," he says, and I nod, pulling him in for a hug.

"How have you been?" I ask him as we head inside.

"Fine."

That's Theo for you. He's always fine. My dad would have loved him. He never shows emotion, never lets on to what's really happening to him inside.

We head to a booth towards the back, and I slide in across from him.

"So, what's up?" He asks as we each grab a menu.

"Nothing," I lie.

"Then why did you call me to meet you at three o'clock in the morning?"

"Can't I just miss you?"

"No," he states flatly, and I roll my eyes.

"I slept with Lottie."

"Fucking finally!" He half shouts, and I stare at him in shock.

The waitress chooses that moment to come over and take our order. She gives us a sleepy smile as she flips open her notepad.

"Pancakes and coffee please," I order.

"Same, but add bacon to mine."

She nods, turning to head back behind the counter.

"You knew that I liked Lottie?" I ask once she's gone.

"Liked?" he asks sarcastically, and I kick him under the table.

He glares at me, and I roll my eyes.

My phone buzzes, and I pull it out, noticing that I have a text from Rhett and three unread emails. Guilt hits me when I see Rhett's name on the screen, and I avoid it, opening up my emails instead.

"Shit," I grumble, and Theo raises an eyebrow in question. "I got assigned a training this week."

"Bummer," he says in that monotone voice of his.

"It really is. I'm going to be stuck sleeping in a tent and running on the beach for like a week."

"Get back to the interesting part of tonight," he says, and I flick him off.

"I slept with Lottie."

"Congrats," he deadpans.

"I think that it was a mistake."

"Why?"

"We didn't really talk about it. We had both been drinking. What if she regrets it? Rhett is going to murder me."

"She won't, and neither will he," he says, and he sounds so sure.

"How do you know?"

"Because I know all three of you."

I want to trust Theo, but what does he know? He's barely seen Lottie in the last few years, and he's never had a real relationship.

The waitress comes back with our food, and we both dig in. Theo leaves me alone to my thoughts, and I appreciate that. Sometimes it's nice to just sit in silence with someone.

I try to work through what my options are. I don't have many. I need to go back home and get my things so I can report to base in a few hours.

Should I wake her up when I get back?

Should I leave a note or just text her?

Maybe having a week away from her will do me some good. I can try to figure out my next steps then.

"I need to get back to the office," Theo says, and I side-eye him.

"It's four am. You need to go to bed."

"That's how they win."

"Who?" I ask with a laugh as we slide out of the booth.

He just gives me one of his rare smiles before we head for the door. Theo might come across as a stuck-up prick, and to some extent, he is, but he's also a good guy with a wicked sense of humor.

I wave goodbye to him and climb behind the wheel to make the short drive home.

By the time I get there, though, I still have no idea what to do now.

FIVE

Lottie

"HOW ARE YOU DOING?" Goldie asks.

She's been using her calm tone on me for the last few weeks. I hate it. It just reminds me of how fragile I'm feeling right now.

It's been close to four weeks since Anson and I slept together, and then he disappeared. I had woken up feeling so hopeful about our future. I knew we would have a lot to talk about and discuss, but I was ready. We were finally on the same page.

Except we weren't.

I woke up alone, and at first, I thought maybe he was in the shower or had slipped out to grab breakfast. Only, he never came back home.

I tried to call him at least a dozen times, but he never answered any of them. My texts went unanswered as well.

After a few days of radio silence, it hit me that he was

ghosting me. All the hope and excitement I had been feeling was long gone. Now I'm just feeling empty.

And really pissed off.

I can't believe that Anson would do this. I can't believe that he would just abandon me like that.

I keep swinging from rage to despair, and it's starting to wear on me. I haven't been sleeping very well lately. I'm so stressed out that I'm sick to my stomach. I've even thrown up a few times in the last couple of days.

"I'm fine," I tell Goldie, but I know neither of us is buying that.

"Lottie," Goldie starts.

"I just feel like I lost him. It's like I threw away over a decade of friendship for one night, and I don't know if it was worth it," I say, fresh tears starting to spill down my cheeks.

"Why don't we hang out tonight?" Goldie suggests. "We can drink and cry together."

"What's wrong?" Boss Man asks, and Goldie sighs.

"This is a private conversation."

"Why are you going to cry?"

"Because I work for you."

"Hilarious," Boss Man deadpans.

"I'll let you get back to work."

"But tonight?"

"I'm in. Come over here?"

"Perfect. I'll see you around six."

I hang up and go back to staring blankly at my computer screen. I threw myself into work when Anson first left, trying to distract myself, and managed to finish all my projects for the rest of the month. Now that I'm ahead, though, I can't seem to find the will to work.

I just want to take a nap.

I wipe the tears from my cheeks and wrap the blanket tighter around my shoulders. My stomach protests, and I bolt for the bathroom, making it just in time to throw up the toast I ate for breakfast.

I brush my teeth, splashing some cold water on my face before I trudge back to the bedroom and collapse onto the bed.

I grab my phone, texting Goldie as my eyes start to droop.

LOTTIE: We might want to cancel. I haven't been feeling so great the last few days. Wouldn't want you to get sick.

MY FINGER HOVERS over the message thread with Anson, and I bite my lip. I've given up on reaching him, but I can't stop rereading our latest messages. It's like I love torturing myself.

My phone rings with a FaceTime call, and I force a smile to my face as I answer my brother's call.

"Hey! How are you doing?" I ask him.

I've learned to beat him to the punch in our last few calls. I need to direct the conversation; otherwise Rhett will bring up Anson, and then I have to really work to avoid that subject.

"Good. How about you? You look a little pale," Rhett says, concern etched all over his face.

"Yeah, I think that I might have the flu or something. I was just about to take a nap, actually," I tell him, and he nods.

"Is Anson taking care of you?"

My stomach drops, and I feel like throwing up again.

"Yeah, he just ran to get me some Gatorade," I lie, and Rhett nods.

"I haven't been able to get ahold of him," he says, and I swallow hard.

"Yeah, his phone is messed up. I think it might still be turned off or something from his deployment."

"Well, tell him to call the store and get his phone unfrozen so I can call him."

"I will."

There I go. Another lie. I'm really on a roll here.

I hate lying to my brother. He's the only family I have and he means the world to me. We've always been honest with each other, even when it was hard, but I just can't tell him what happened. Not right now.

I've been telling myself that it's because I'm worried about him being stressed or distracted while he's over there, but really, I just don't know how to broach the subject or what to even say.

"Well, feel better soon, okay? I'm going out tomorrow so I'll be out of range for a few days," he tells me.

"Be safe."

"You know I will."

I swallow, fighting off another round of tears. I'm scared for my brother, worried that something bad will happen. I'm relieved that I won't have to answer any more questions about Anson for a few days, and thinking that just makes me feel guilty.

"Get some rest, Lot. I'll talk to you in a few days."

"Thanks. Be safe. Good luck."

I give him a watery smile, and he waves, looking worried and grim as we end the call. I close my eyes, rubbing my forehead, and my phone dings with a new message.

. . .

GOLDIE: I hate to say this, but have you thought about taking a pregnancy test?
   Lottie: What?
   Goldie: I mean, it could just be stress or whatever but with the timing of everything...

SHE DOESN'T FINISH that sentence, but she doesn't need to.

LOTTIE: Fuck.
   Goldie: Yep.
   Goldie: I'll pick up a few tests on my way over.
   Lottie: What am I going to do?
   Goldie: We'll figure it out. I promise.

I ROLL over onto my back, staring up at the ceiling as I wonder what I'll do if I really am pregnant. I can't wait until tonight to find out so I toss off the covers and head down the street to the corner shop.

My palms are sweaty as I grab two different brands of pregnancy tests and make my way up to the counter. The girl ringing me up gives me a weak smile as she scans the items and takes my cash.

"Thanks," I mumble as I grab the bag and head back to my apartment.

I feel like I'm going to throw up again as I rip open the first box and pull out the test. I read the instructions twice, my hands shaking with nerves the entire time, and then I'm peeing on a stick and trying not to throw up.

It feels like the longest three minutes of my life as I wait to see if there will be one line or two. I pace back and forth in the tiny bathroom, wringing my hands together as I wait for the timer to go off.

When it does, I don't feel ready to look at the results.

You have to know. Come on, Lottie. You're a big girl.

I take a deep breath before I step up to the bathroom counter and look down at the test.

Two lines.

Two freaking lines.

My legs give out, and I sink down to the floor.

I'm pregnant.

I'm pregnant, and I can't get my baby daddy to respond to my calls.

What the hell am I supposed to do now?

SIX

Anson

I'M IN HELL.

I thought that lusting after Lottie but never having her was torture, but it's paradise compared to this.

Lottie stopped trying to reach out to me a while ago, and I thought that would make things easier, but I miss her. At least when she was calling and texting me, I knew she was thinking about me. Now, who knows?

I've been lying awake at night, wondering if Lottie is missing me. Is she mad at me? Is she crying? Has she moved on to someone else?

It's the not knowing that's driving me crazy.

"You look like hell," Theo says as he slides into the other side of the booth.

"So do you. Still pining after your assistant?" I ask him, trying to change the subject.

We've been meeting up at least once a week to catch up. I spent the first two times telling him all about Lottie and what happened with her. He thinks I should just man up and tell her that I love her, but he's a known asshole, so I'm not sure I should take his advice.

Besides, it's not just clearing things up with Lottie. I have to think about Rhett and our friendship too.

Lottie probably doesn't even want me anymore. Not after I've spent the last three weeks ghosting her.

I was supposed to come up with a plan and go back to the apartment, but that never quite happened. I've been crashing with Theo and a few guys on base, couch surfing until... well, I don't know when I'll go back to the apartment.

I've had to buy new clothes and toiletries because I was too much of a coward to go back to the apartment and face her. I just needed time to figure stuff out, but it's been weeks, and I still don't have anything cleared up.

"I'm not in love with Clara," Theo grumbles, grabbing the sticky menu and glaring at it like it's wronged him.

"Right."

I don't believe him one bit. I'm good at reading people, and I can see the look in his eyes when he talks about her. He took a call from her last week, and I swear his whole face softened. Obviously, he loves her, but I guess he won't admit that yet.

"Have you talked to your girl yet?" He asks, and I grab my own menu.

"No," I grumble.

"Why don't you just call her?" He suggests.

As if on cue, my phone rings, and I tense when I see Lottie's name on the screen.

"That's her, isn't it," Theo says, and I grit my teeth as I shove my phone back into my pocket.

I wonder why she's reaching out now. What's changed?

"Why don't you answer it?"

"Not yet."

He rolls his eyes, and I go back to ignoring him as I study the menu.

"When are you going to face her?" Theo snaps, and I grind my teeth together.

The truth is that I don't know. I'm too guilty, too disgusted with myself to face her now. What kind of man sleeps with a girl and then ghosts her? An asshole, that's who.

I'm caving, though.

I miss her. I miss her sense of humor and her smiles. I miss talking to her and hearing about her day.

Our waitress stops by, and we order the same thing that we've gotten every other time we come here. She just gives us a tired nod before she shuffles away, and I grab a napkin, shredding it as I wrestle with my thoughts.

I need to man up already and face the music. The longer that I wait, the worse it will be when I face her.

I've been ducking Rhett's phone calls, too, and I know that he's caught on that something isn't right.

"I have work to do back at the office," Theo says when I straighten in my seat.

It seems he's better at reading people than I gave him credit for.

"You know if you wanted to go and fix things with your girl."

"You're just anxious to get back to your assistant," I tell him, and he rolls his eyes.

My phone rings again, and this time I'm going to answer Lottie's call.

Except it isn't Lottie calling.

"Excuse me," I say, sliding out of the booth as I hit answer.

"Hello?"

"Mr. Lark?"

"Yes?"

"This is Dr. Tuller calling from the Veterans Hospital."

Just like that, my stomach drops.

"Rhett," I choke out, and he clears his throat.

"Yes, Rhett was injured while on duty. He's just arrived here, and you were listed as one of his emergency contacts."

"Is he okay?" I ask, my stomach tied up in knots.

"He's stable."

"I'll be there in twenty," I tell him before I hang up.

"Rhett's been injured," I tell Theo, and he nods.

"Let's go."

He throws a hundred down on the table, and we both race out of the diner and over to his car. He drove both of us here today so I don't have my car.

"What happened?" He asks, and I pause.

"I don't know. They just said that he was injured but stable."

Theo nods, and I turn to stare out the passenger window. I wonder if Lottie knows yet. I wonder how she's taking it.

Looks like I'm about to find out soon enough.

SEVEN

Lottie

WHEN MY PHONE RINGS, I tense up. My first thought is that it's Anson finally calling me back, and I'm just not sure I'm ready to face him. I know I've been trying to get ahold of him since I found out that I was pregnant, but I've secretly been happy that he's still ducking my calls and texts.

I take a deep breath before I glance at the screen, and then I relax when I see that it's not him. It's an unknown number, and I figure that it's a new client calling me so I answer, forcing myself to sound cheerful.

"Hello, this is Lottie St. James."

"Ms. St. James, this is Dr. Tuller at the Veterans Hospital."

My stomach drops, and it starts to sound like everything is underwater. I struggle to take a deep breath, trying to calm my racing heart and organize my thoughts.

"Is it Anson or Rhett?" I blurt out.

"Rhett was brought in," Dr. Tuller says, and I gasp, dropping to my knees at his words.

I'm sobbing, trembling, my arms wrapped around my stomach as I rock back and forth on my knees.

"Ms. St. James? Ms. St. James?" Dr. Tuller asks, and I take a deep breath.

I have to know what happened. I have to know if he's okay.

"Is he okay? Is my brother okay?"

"He's stable. Rhett was injured while on duty, and he just arrived here at the hospital, but he's stable."

"Oh, thank god."

I sag back against the wall, my heart pounding in my ears as I try to calm down.

"I'll be there in twenty," I tell the doctor before I hang up and rise to my feet shakily.

My hand is still wrapped around my stomach, and I realize I was scared that my baby would never meet his uncle.

I wonder if Anson knows that Rhett's been injured. I'm pretty sure he's one of Rhett's emergency contacts, too, so I'm sure he was called.

I wonder if he bothered to pick up.

My phone rings again, and this time it's Goldie.

"Hey, how's my baby mama?" She jokes when I answer.

"Rhett's been injured. He's in the Veteran's Hospital now," I blurt out.

"I'll meet you there."

She hangs up, and I start to feel better, knowing that I'm not going to have to see Rhett all alone.

I gather my things, my sweater, purse, can of ginger ale, and a few pregnancy pops before I head out the door. I'm still shaking a little, but the hospital isn't too far away. I slip behind the wheel, trying to concentrate as I start the car and back out of my spot.

"It's going to be okay, little one. Uncle Rhett is a fighter. He'll be alright," I murmur to my stomach.

The morning sickness has been really rough this week. I've gone through a case of ginger ale already. I ordered the pregnancy pops on day two, and I'm almost done with the box. I'll need to buy more if I want to survive this first trimester.

I've been reading more about babies and pregnancies, and now I'm just looking forward to the second trimester when I hopefully won't be so exhausted or sick.

I keep talking to my little bean on the short drive to the hospital and by the time I arrive, I've almost calmed down.

By the time I've parked and made it up to the front door, Goldie is already waiting there. She rushes to my side when she spots me and throws her arms around me.

"Are you okay? What did they tell you?" She asks me, and I wrap my arms around her.

"Just that he was injured while on duty but that he's stable."

"Well, that's good, right?"

"I don't know. I need to see him."

She nods, wrapping her arm around my shoulders and leading me into the hospital. She marches right up to the front desk and asks for Rhett's room number.

"Are you family?" The nurse asks.

"Yes, we're his sisters," Goldie lies, but we look enough alike that she doesn't question her.

"Room 314."

As soon as we get the room number, we rush toward the elevators and wait impatiently for the doors to open. We step on, and Goldie hits the button for the third floor.

Nerves start hitting me as I wonder what kind of shape Rhett will be in.

I'm staring out the elevator doors when a familiar face catches my eye.

"Anson," I whisper when I see him rush into the hospital with a frantic look on his face.

I don't know if he senses me staring at him, but he turns, and for the first time in weeks, our eyes lock.

He looks tired and worn down. There are dark circles under his eyes, and I wonder where he's been staying.

"Do you want me to hold the door?" Goldie asks as Anson turns and heads our way, and I shake my head.

"Hell no."

"Good girl," Goldie says, and I'm sure she's flipping Anson off as the elevator doors close and we're ushered up to the third floor.

I feel like I've been thrown out into a hurricane. I don't know what to focus on or how to get through this. I'm about to see Rhett and have to deal with how injured he is. I'm about to see Anson for the first time in weeks. I'm going to have to tell both of them that I'm pregnant.

I don't know how to deal with any of this.

Goldie pauses outside of Rhett's room, and I swallow hard.

"Are you ready?" She asks, squeezing my hand, and I nod.

I'm blinking back tears before I even walk into the room, and I lose the battle when I see my brother lying in that hospital bed.

"Oh, Rhett," I sob, and he blinks his eyes open, giving me a tired smile.

"Hey, Lot."

I rush to his side, and he tries to sit up more in the bed.

"I'm fine," he promises, and I glare at him.

"Obviously."

"I really am," he assures me. "I got off easy. It could have been a lot worse."

"Glad that you're okay," Goldie says, giving him a smile.

"Hey, Goldie. How have you been?"

"Good. Keeping busy."

"Yeah, you and your boss manage to get on the same page yet?"

"Nope."

"Figures," he says with a laugh.

He shifts in the bed, and I see him wince. I know then that it's worse than he's pretending.

"What happened?" I ask him, though I'm not sure I want to know all the details.

"We were attacked while we were out on patrol. A bomb went off, and I got thrown back into this building... and then shot."

"Jesus, Rhett," I sob, and he squeezes my hand.

"I'm alright. They patched me up. I'm going to be fine."

I sigh, and he squeezes my hand again.

"Where's Anson?" He asks.

"He's coming up now."

"Yeah? What's going on with you two? You've both been weird ever since he got back to the states."

"Nothing," I spit out, but even I can hear the bitterness in my tone.

"Did something finally happen between you two?" Rhett asks, and I blink.

"What? What do you mean?" I ask, my voice wobbling.

"I mean that I've always known that you two love each other. It's been obvious since we were kids, but Anson has too much honor to do something about it. He thinks that he's going to hurt me by going after you."

I want to laugh at Anson having honor, but I manage to hold myself back.

"I don't mind, though. Anson is a good guy, and I trust him. I know that he would never hurt you."

I swallow hard, staring at the far wall.

"I love you both. I just want both of you to be happy," Rhett says, and I see Goldie shift.

She's obviously uncomfortable with being here for this conversation. I'm not sure what to say back to Rhett.

Do I tell him that we did sleep together, and then Anson said fuck his honor and disappeared? Do I tell him that I'm pregnant?

I'm saved from having to answer by the hospital door opening and Anson rushing in.

EIGHT

Anson

SEEING Lottie again is like a kick in the gut.

I thought that I would be in charge the next time that I faced her. I thought that I would be calm and have a solid plan. Instead, it's happening on the most stressful day of my life. I'm not calm or in control of anything right now.

When she didn't hold the elevator, I knew that she was pissed. I could see it on her face. Her eyes were hard, filled with fury.

I know that I hurt her. I know that I fucked up. The worst part is that I don't even have a good excuse. I just panicked and didn't know how to fix any of this. I still don't.

I was upset with myself for betraying Rhett, and that's all that I could think about after I slept with Lottie. I was so wrapped up in feeling like an asshole to my oldest friend that I pulled back from the girl of my dreams. By doing so, I fucked up with Lottie.

I don't want to hurt Rhett or ruin our friendship, but I

think I did that when I slept with his little sister. I never wanted to hurt Lottie, but I did that when I slept with her and then disappeared. Either way, I did the one thing I never wanted to do and hurt both of them.

I don't think I could have won or gotten away without hurting one of them, but I've realized that I should have chosen Lottie. I can't live without her, especially not now that I've had her. I need her in my life. I've learned that in the last few weeks.

I take a deep breath as I walk into Rhett's room with Theo hot on my heels. He had dropped me off at the door while he parked the car, but by the time I figured out Rhett's room number, he had caught up to me.

"Hey," I greet the room as I walk in, my eyes straying to Lottie before they lock on Rhett. "How are you doing?"

"I'm fine. Really," he says, giving Lottie a look when she steps closer to him.

Being face-to-face with Rhett just brings everything to the forefront for me. I know I will need to come clean and tell him that I slept with his sister. Should I do it now, though? Or wait until he's on the mend more and at least out of the hospital.

Once again, I'm back to that weird state where it feels like I'm not on solid ground. I'm used to having a plan. I'm used to getting orders, following a plan of attack, and things running smoothly. It's part of the reason why I love the military. It's the complete opposite of my childhood, and I've grown used to the routine of that career, and I miss it now that I'm in this situation.

I look over to Lottie again, and I can't put my finger on it, but Lottie seems different. She looks tired, and guilt starts to eat away at me. Has she been feeling alright since I left? She seems pale, and I wonder if she's been feeling sick.

I should have been there for her.

Self-disgust and guilt gnaw at me as I move to the other side of Rhett's bed. He's hooked up to so many monitors and the annoying but comforting beep of the heart monitor fills the room.

"What have the doctors said?" I ask, stealing another glance at Lottie, but her gaze is firmly on her brother.

"I don't remember much. I was on a lot of pain medicine when I got here, and it was just the nurse who was in here when I woke up a few minutes ago," Rhett says.

He keeps looking between Lottie and me, and I start to tense up.

"I'll go find the doctor," Theo says, and I jump.

I had forgotten that he was there at all, and when I turn around, he's already halfway out the door.

"I'm surprised that Theo came," Rhett comments, and I swallow.

"I was with him at lunch when I got the call," I explain, and he nods.

Theo and the doctor come back in before I can try to think of what to say next.

"A full house in here," he says as he starts to flip through Rhett's file.

I can see Lottie swaying on her feet, and I can't take it anymore. I move over to her side of the bed, putting a steadying hand on her waist as we wait to hear what the doctor has to say. She tenses against me, and I want to punch myself in the face for hurting her.

"I'm sorry," I whisper in her ear, and she shakes her head.

"So, the scans all came back okay. You'll be sore for some time now from the broken ribs and gunshot wound. We're going to keep you for another day at least, but then you should be cleared to go home. You'll be off duty for a while. We'll need to rehab your shoulder," he says, and Rhett nods.

Lottie takes a step away from me and closer to Rhett, and I feel lost without her by my side.

God, I've been such an idiot. I thought I needed to have everything perfect before I could go back to her, but that was never going to happen. I needed to pick a side. I needed to pick a side years ago.

I should have manned up a decade ago and told them both how much she meant to me, but I didn't. I've fucked this thing up between us since we were kids, and now, I've probably lost the girl of my dreams forever.

"Visiting hours are ending soon," Dr. Tuller says before he heads for the door.

"We'll let you get some rest. I'll be back first thing in the morning, though," Lottie promises him, and I nod.

"We both will," I say, and Rhett nods.

I can tell that he's tired. His eyelids keep drooping, and I'm sure they have him on quite a bit of pain medicine that's making him loopy.

I follow Goldie, Theo, and Lottie out, and we head over to the elevator. I give Theo a look, and he sighs, rolling his eyes but nodding, and I know that he's going to stall Goldie so that I can talk to Lottie alone.

The elevator comes, and I step on with Lottie. Theo turns to Goldie, clearing his throat and grabbing her arm before she can get on.

"Don't you work next door? At the Miller Building?" He asks her, and she blinks as the elevator doors close.

Lottie turns, moving to the furthest corner from me.

"Lottie, I—" I start, and she glares at me.

The elevator doors open, and she bolts, beelining for the front door.

"Lottie, wait! Just let me explain!" I call after her as she zigzags across the parking lot toward her car.

I catch up with her, wrapping my hand around her bicep and pulling her to a stop before she can get into her car.

"Please, Lottie. Just let me explain," I beg.

"Now you want to talk?" She spits at me, and I swallow hard.

"I'm sorry. I deserve that. I just... I panicked."

She laughs then, the sound coming out bitter and full of anger.

"I just needed to get it straight in my head," I try again.

"And did you? Did you figure it out in your head in the last *three* weeks?" She snaps.

"I... I'm sorry," I say lamely.

I have no real defense for what I've done to her. I don't know what to say to make any of this right, and it's killing me.

"Lottie, I'm so sorry."

"You keep saying that. I wish that you would just stop."

She looks away from me, and I can see her blinking back tears as she looks over toward the busy highway.

This isn't where I wanted to have this conversation. This isn't how I wanted this conversation to go at all.

"I've always wanted you, Anson. I've always loved you, and I thought, I thought that we were finally on the same page, but then you left me. You just left in the middle of the night, and then you shut me out. How do you think it felt to wake up alone and then realize that you ghosted me?"

Tears sting my eyes, and I want to pull her against me

when I see she's crying. She looks so hurt and exhausted, and I hate myself. I hate what I've done to her, to us.

"You left me, and I needed you, but I can't keep doing this anymore. I can't keep pining after you anymore."

She starts to cry then, and I want to sink to my knees and beg her to forgive me, to give me a second chance. I'm afraid to let go of her, though. I know that she'll try to run as soon as she can.

"Lottie, I know you don't want to hear it, but I am sorry. I just freaked out. I never wanted to hurt you or Rhett, and after we slept together, I just kept thinking about how Rhett would take the news. I shouldn't have left. I shouldn't have, and if I could do it all over again, I wouldn't have."

"Wouldn't have what? Slept with me or left?" She snaps, and I open my mouth to answer.

She rips her arm out of my grip and climbs into her car. I try to catch the door, but it slams in my face. She starts the car and rolls the window down, giving me a brittle smile.

"You're going to really regret our night together after this," she says, and I frown.

"I don't regret it. I –"

"I'm pregnant."

Those words hit me like a bomb, and my mouth drops open as I stare at her.

"Where's your honor now?" She mumbles, and I reach for the car window, but she shifts into reverse and drives off.

I stand there, gaping after her until her car disappears from view.

What the hell am I supposed to do now?

I can't keep going on like this. It was already wearing on me, and now that Lottie is pregnant, it's time for me to make a choice.

And I choose Lottie.

I can't take it anymore. I'd been walking away or watching this girl walk away from me for way too long.

I turn on my heel and rush back into the hospital. I know that visiting hours are almost over, but I'll just have to convince them to make an exception in my case.

I take the elevator up to the third floor, slipping down the hallway when the nurses are distracted and heading into Rhett's room.

"We need to talk," I say once the door is closed behind me.

"About what's going on between you and Lottie?" He guesses, and I nod.

I swallow hard. I've been so scared of messing this up and losing the only family that I have left, and I know that I need to play this right.

"Yeah. I'm in love with her, Rhett."

"Dude, I know," he says, shocking the hell out of me.

"You know?" I half shout, and he rolls his eyes.

"I think that everyone knows that you two love each other. Except maybe the two of you."

"Well..." I start but his telling me that he already knows is kind of taking the wind out of my sails.

"Have you two finally gotten together? Did you have a fight?" Rhett asks, trying to sit up in the bed more.

"We, uh, we slept together and then, well."

Well, this is awkward.

"I don't need to know all of the deals. I'm guessing that you did something to mess it up?"

"Yeah, I panicked. I thought you would hate me, and I've kind of been avoiding her for the last few weeks."

"That explains why she's so pissed at you," he says with a sigh, and I nod.

"I really messed up."

"Yeah, you did," he says. "What are you going to do now?"

"I'm going to fix this. I'm going to make her mine."

"Good," he says with a nod and a wide smile. "Now go get her."

NINE

Lottie

WELL, now the tables sure have turned.

It's been three days, and I'm doing my best to avoid Anson. He's back to work on base by now, and I know his schedule so I've been going to see Rhett during the day and leaving by three so there's no way I'll have to face Anson.

That hasn't stopped him from calling and texting about a million times. I've been ducking all of his calls and refusing to even open his texts.

Goldie thinks that I should hear him out, but I just can't bring myself to face him. Not yet, anyway. I've been staying with her for the last three days because I wasn't sure if Anson would try to come by the apartment or not.

Rhett was kept longer at the hospital, but he should be getting released today, and I know I'll need to face Anson now.

My time of avoiding him is about to be over.

I place a hand on my stomach, trying to ignore the

nausea. I had a few saltines before I came here, hoping it would help settle my stomach, but they don't seem to be doing the trick.

I step off the elevator and let out a yelp when I'm immediately pushed back on.

"What are you doing?" I snap at Anson as the doors close behind him.

"We need to talk."

"I don't want to talk to you now."

"You need to. I'm sorry, Lottie. Just hear me out. Please," he says, and I look away from him, my hands fisting at my sides as I mull over his request.

"Rhett is getting one last scan. He's not in his room right now anyway," he adds, and I sigh.

"Fine. Let's get this over with."

The elevator opens, and we step off together.

"Where are we doing this?" I ask him.

"There's a diner across the street."

I nod, and he takes my elbow, steering me outside and down the block. We head into the diner, and he leads me over to a booth in the back.

"Can I get you something to drink?" The waitress asks in a bored tone.

"Ginger ale," I say right away, and Anson frowns.

I never used to be able to stand ginger ale or even Sprite, but I can't seem to stop drinking it now.

"Pregnancy. Morning sickness," I tell him, and understanding dawns on him.

He ducks his head, looking ashamed that he didn't already know that, and I glance back out the window and over to the Veteran's Hospital.

"Just a water, please."

She nods, ambling away, and I look back to Anson.

"So?"

"I can not tell you how sorry I am, Lottie."

"You've told me."

"I know, but that doesn't make up for what happened. I handled all of this all wrong. I'm not used to being in situations like this. You were... you were my first, and it was the best moment of my life... until I thought about telling Rhett."

I swallow hard. I've been trying not to think about our night together that much, but I have to admit that I never once thought about things from his perspective.

"I didn't know that you were a virgin, too," I whisper, and he nods.

"I've only ever wanted you, Lot. No one else was ever good enough."

I can feel myself softening towards him, but I can't have that. He disappeared for weeks. He doesn't get to just say sorry and everything goes back to normal. I steel my spine, straightening my shoulders as I try to stare him down.

"I know that it might not seem like it after what happened," he continues, and I snort.

"We were friends. We were *family*," I stress. "And you ghosted me!"

"I know. I'm not explaining this right at all. I really did panic. I was afraid that you were going to wake up and say that you were drunk and you'd be upset that we slept together, maybe even regret it. Then Rhett would be pissed at me too. I thought I was going to lose both of you, and I guess I ran so I wouldn't have to face that happening."

"It wouldn't have."

"I know that now," he says. "I almost came back that night, but by the time I worked up the courage, I had to report to base. I wasn't intentionally avoiding you that first week. I was in training and barely had time to eat or sleep. I swear," he says, and I nod.

"That doesn't explain all of the other weeks, though," I point out, and he sighs.

"I just... it was like too much time had passed. I didn't know how to make any of it right."

The waitress comes back, dropping off our drinks. She takes one look at us and doesn't bother asking if we're ready to order. I wonder if she can sense the tension between us and is figuring it's not worth it.

"How's the pregnancy? How have you been feeling?" He asks, trying to change the subject.

I can see that he's nervous to ask, but he looks excited about the baby. I start to soften towards him again, and I grit my teeth. I'm not forgiving him that easily.

"The morning sickness has been rough."

He nods, seeming so excited about our future together, and that's when I start to get really angry.

He's acting like everything is fine between us. Like he can just say sorry and we'll go back to... well, to whatever.

Maybe it's the baby hormones or maybe I'm just over-tired. Either way, I find myself fisting my hands under the table and glaring at him.

"What's the plan here, Anson? What do you want from me?"

He opens his mouth, but I steamroll over him.

"You didn't want to have anything to do with me these last few weeks, but now you're all over me because I'm pregnant? If you didn't want me before, then I don't want you now," I snap.

With that, I grab my purse, slide out of the booth and stomp toward the exit.

TEN

Anson

I CAN'T KEEP DOING this. I need to tell her that I'm so sorry and would do anything to fix all of this.

I toss a twenty on the table and rush after my girl. She's about halfway across the parking lot when I catch up with her.

"No, stop," I say as I wrap my hand around her wrist and tug her to stop and turn to face me. "I love you, Lottie."

She freezes, her body tensing as she stares at me with those big pale blue eyes of hers.

"I'm an idiot, Lottie. I've been in love with you for years and trying to balance my friendship with you and Rhett with my feelings for you, and I blew it all up in one night: I should have chosen you."

She blinks, her wrist hanging limply in my grasp.

"I should have chosen you that night. I should have chosen you ten years ago. You mean more to me than my friendship with Rhett, and I can't live without you. I've tried to the last few weeks, and it fucking sucked."

She looks away from me, staring at the cracked sidewalk beneath our feet.

"I was just scared that I was going to lose the only family I've ever known. I shouldn't have pushed you away, and I'll hate myself every day for not waking up next to you the next morning. I've messed all of this up between us, but I swear that if you give me a second chance, I'll make up for all of this. I'll do anything you ask to make this right, baby."

"Are you just saying that because I'm pregnant?" She asks, her eyes watery with unshed tears.

"Fuck no! I promise I'll stop swearing so much before the baby is here," I rush to add, and she laughs.

A car honks, and I realize that we're blocking the parking lot's exit so I drag her over to the sidewalk.

"I love you, Lottie. I've wanted you from the second that I saw you. I loved you when I didn't even know what love was. I would want you and love you even if you weren't pregnant with our kid. Please, baby. Please give me a second chance to make this right for you."

She chews on her plump bottom lip, and I hold my breath. She has my heart resting in her hands, and if she broke it right now, I would deserve that. It doesn't stop me from hoping that she doesn't.

"Okay," she finally whispers, and my knees almost buckle with relief.

"Really?" I can't help but ask, and she laughs.

"Should I say no?"

"No! I love you," I say, gathering her up in my arms before she can change her mind.

"I love you too," she whispers in my ear, and I tighten my grip on her, nearly crushing her against me.

"The baby," she wheezes, and I release her.

"Oh my god! I'm going to get better at this. I'll read all the books," I promise her as my hands go to her stomach.

"We're okay," she assures me, and I relax slightly. "What happens now?"

"Well, we need to tell Rhett, and I'd like to take you out on a proper date. When you're up for it," I add, remembering that she said her morning sickness was rough.

"I have a doctor's appointment this afternoon. Do you want to come with—"

"Yes."

She laughs, giving me one of those smiles that I love so much.

"Maybe I can take you out to dinner after?" I ask, not wanting to push my luck too much.

"Maybe," she says with a smile.

She takes my hand in hers, and I feel like the luckiest man alive as she leads me back to the hospital and up to Rhett's room.

When we walk into his room holding hands, he just grins.

"It's about damn time, you two!"

Lottie just leans against my side, and I smile down at her.

"We have one more surprise for you," I start, and she looks up at me.

"I'm pregnant."

Rhett tries to jump up to give us a hug, and the nurse glares at him until he sits back down.

"That's awesome! Congratulations, you two!"

I let go of Lottie so she can hug her brother, and I'm right behind her.

"Are you ready to get out of here?" I ask him, and he chuckles.

"So ready."

The nurse glares at him again, and he holds up his hands.

"Not that I haven't loved the care here. It's the bed," he promises her, and she rolls her eyes before she heads out of his room.

"Making friends, I see," I quip, and he laughs.

I grab his bag, and the nurse comes back in with a wheelchair.

"I'm going to go bring the car around," Lottie tells us, and Rhett nods to her.

"Go help your girl," he tells me.

I glance between him and the nurse, biting back my knowing grin before I head out after Lottie. I catch up with her before she can get on the elevator and she sighs, leaning into my side.

"What time's the doctor's appointment? Maybe you can get a nap in," I say, brushing her hair back from her face.

"No, we'll have to drop Rhett off at home, make sure that he's situated, and then head back out."

I rub circles on her back as we ride down to the first floor and then over to her car.

"Do you want me to drive?" I ask her.

"Where's your truck?"

"Over there, but I'm not sure that Rhett can get in and out of that very easily," I point out, and she nods.

"Why don't you follow us home then? You can drive us to the doctor's appointment."

"Sounds good."

I lean down, brushing my lips across hers, and it feels so natural. It's not enough, not nearly enough, but we're in the crowded hospital parking lot, and I know it's not the place to make out.

I pull back, giving her one last smile before I walk over to my truck and climb in. I watch her back out and go to the front to pick Rhett up, and then we're turning out of the parking lot and towards home.

Home, I think with a big smile.

ELEVEN

Lottie

ANSON and I are doing this all wrong, but it's perfect.

I've waited years to be with him, and now it's finally happening. He's finally mine.

He can't seem to stop touching me. He keeps looking over and smiling at me like he can't believe that I'm really there. I know the feeling well. I feel like I need to constantly touch him or he'll disappear like a mirage.

"Is this your first doctor's appointment?" He asks me as we turn into the parking lot.

"Yeah, they were a little backed up. I guess one of the doctors retired, and they were trying to work out the schedule so this was the first available date."

He nods, parking in the first open spot and hopping out. He rushes around to my side of the truck and lifts me out like I weigh nothing.

"Are you sure Rhett is going to be okay at home by

himself?" I ask as he takes my hand, and we walk up to the front door.

"Yeah, we left him with like a dozen pillows and the remote. Besides, as long as it's not that hospital bed, I think he's happy."

I smile at that. He was complaining about the hospital bed the entire drive home so I'm sure he's glad to be back in his own bed. They gave us his medicine, too, so I know he'll probably be sleeping for the rest of the afternoon. It doesn't stop me from worrying about him.

Anson stands beside me as I check in and then wraps his arm around my shoulder when we sit to fill out the forms.

"Are you nervous?" He whispers to me, and I look up at him.

"A little. I'm just not sure what to expect, you know?"

He nods, his fingers starting to rub my shoulder.

"It will be okay. I'll be there if you need anything," he promises, and I know he will.

He's been so much lighter ever since we told Rhett and got everything cleared up. I know he'll be apologizing and trying to make up for the last few weeks for the rest of our lives, but I'm truly over it. I just want to focus on our baby now.

"Ms. St. James?" The nurse calls, and I see Anson frown.

"What?" I whisper to him, and he looks at me.

"St. James. We'll have to fix that."

It takes me a minute to comprehend what he's saying. and then I gape at him.

"Did you just propose to me in the OBGYN office?" I blurt out, and he laughs.

"No, when I propose to you, it will be a little more romantic than that."

He wraps his arm around my shoulders, and we follow the nurse back to our room. I can tell that she overheard us and is trying not to laugh as we go, and it makes me relax.

"We'll be getting our first look at the baby today," she explains once she's taken all of my vitals, and I nod and my heart starts to race.

Anson must be able to sense the nerves because he steps closer to me, taking my hand in his.

"You'll have to strip from the waist down and lay back on the table. You can use this blanket to cover yourself," the nurse says as she starts to get the computer ready. "I'll step out and give you a minute."

I nod, taking a deep breath once she's gone and push my yoga pants down my legs. I hurry to take off my panties and lay down on the table. Anson moves to sit in the chair next to my hand, and we reach for each other at the same time.

"Are you ready for this?" I ask him, and he nods.

"I love you, Lottie," he says as he leans over and kisses my forehead. "We'll get through this together."

I nod, and the nurse comes back into the room. The lights are off, and she moves to the computer again.

"For this first appointment, we need to insert a wand to see the baby. After this though, every other ultrasound will be with the wand on your stomach."

I take a deep breath, staring at the screen as the grainy black image is replaced with a small white circle.

"That's your baby," she says, pointing to a spot on the screen, and Anson's hold on me tightens.

"I'm just going to take some measurements," she says, and I nod distractedly as I stare at our tiny little bean.

The rest of the appointment is a blur. She takes some

pictures, passing them to us before she leaves the room, and then Anson is dragging me into his lap, and we're both staring at the tiny shots of our baby.

"So small," he says, and I nod.

"Seeing it just made it so real," I whisper, and he nods.

He kisses my forehead once more before he helps me get dressed, and then we head up to the counter to make our next appointment. I let Anson handle that as I stare down at the pictures. My phone has been buzzing all afternoon with messages from Goldie, and I know that I'll need to send her pictures of the ultrasound scan soon before she starts calling.

"Are you hungry?" Anson asks as we head back out to his truck.

"Starving."

"What would you like to eat?"

"Nachos and pickles."

"Done."

I laugh, wondering what he has in store for our date tonight. I sit back in the passenger seat, letting him take care of me as we weave in and out of traffic. He makes one stop, running into a little market, and then we're headed toward the beach.

"This place has the best tacos in the whole city," he promises as he leads me to the food truck.

I let him hold my hand as he orders for us, and then we carry our bags of food across the sand and find a secluded spot down by the water.

"Your nachos and pickles," he says, brandishing a jar of pickles from the market bag and my takeout container of nachos from the food truck.

"Thank you!"

I let him open the jar of pickles as I start on the nachos, and I moan.

"This is so good," I tell him, and he grins.

"I know. I found this place the other week and knew I had to bring you here."

There's a moment of awkward silence as he remembers that we weren't talking a few weeks ago, and he clears his throat.

"I really am so sorry for—"

"I know, Anson. It's okay."

"No, it's not."

"Well, it's not okay," I agree, "but you're never going to do it again."

"Never," he promises, and we go back to eating.

The subject changes to lighter topics. He tells me about the training he just got done with, and I laugh as he retells about some guy eating pasta before it started and throwing up after only the first mile of a ten-mile run. He complains about sleeping in a tent with twenty other dudes, and I give him an update on some of my projects and my last girls' night with Goldie.

"She should just ask him out," Anson groans when I tell him that her and Boss Man are still dancing around each other.

"She never will."

"I know. We should do something to set them up, though."

"Steal her phone and text him pretending to be her?" I suggest, and he looks at me with wide eyes.

"Okay, you had that idea ready to go," he says with a laugh, and I blush.

"I just want her to be happy."

"I know, baby. I know."

When the sun starts to set, we gather up all of our trash and walk hand in hand back to his truck. He helps me into the passenger seat, and I stop him before he can close the door.

"You know, typically there's a kiss on first dates and—"

I don't get the rest of the words out before he's pulling me against him, and his lips are claiming mine. My hands land on his shoulders, and I cling to him as his lips slant over mine. Anson's hands find their way into my hair, and he fists the locks, angling my head the way he wants it so that he can claim my mouth further.

My lips part for him when his tongue slips along the seam of my mouth. He deepens the kiss as my tongue starts to tangle with his. His hands fall to my ass, and he tugs me closer to him, and memories from our one and only night together start to flash before my eyes.

I want to feel that way again. I want a do-over of that night.

"Anson," I breathe, gripping his shirt as my body starts to heat with lust. "I want you."

"You have me. You've always had all of me," he tells me in between kisses, and I shake my head.

"I want you to make love to me," I tell him, breaking away from the kiss.

He stares down at me, his eyes dark with love and longing, and I know we're on the same page.

"We can go slow," he starts. "We kind of did all of this backward, but we can go slow."

"What? Do you want to go on more dates and get to know me better?" I ask him. "You already know me better than anyone."

He's breathing hard, and I can see he's fighting with himself.

"I want you, Anson. Now, are you going to take me home and fuck me?" I ask him, throwing down the gauntlet.

"Yes, ma'am."

I grin as he closes the passenger door and sprints around to the other side. When he climbs behind the wheel and we peel out of the parking lot, I can't help but feel lighter and happier than I ever have before.

Our love story might not be the most conventional, we might have done everything backward, but as long as we get our happily ever after ending, then I don't mind.

TWELVE

Anson

WE BOTH CREEP into the apartment, trying to be as quiet as we can, but it's not needed. Rhett is passed out in the living room, the TV on low as he snores away.

Lottie giggles as I grab her hand, and we dash down the hallway to my bedroom. I've been imagining having her in my bed for too long, and now it's finally going to happen.

I close the door behind us quietly, and then I'm on her.

I press her back against the wall, my lips landing on hers as I mold my body against hers. She moans, wrapping her hands around the back of my neck and grinding her hips against mine.

"These baby hormones have been making me so horny," she whispers against my mouth, and I grin.

"I'm happy to help out any way I can," I joke.

"Good. Get naked," she orders, and I nod.

"Yes, ma'am."

I step back, and we both start to strip as fast as humanly

possible. I beat her and drop to my knees, pressing a kiss on her belly before I drape one of her legs over my shoulder and bury my face in her pussy.

"I missed you," I tell her, and she laughs.

"Are you talking to me or my pussy?" She asks, and I laugh.

"Both?"

She smiles down at me, and I lean forward, licking her clit and making her eyes roll back in her head.

"More of that," she says hoarsely, and I nod, happy to oblige.

I get back to work, my tongue moving over her clit as I slip one finger and then two into her drenched channel.

"Such a good girl," I praise her, and her hips start to move to my rhythm.

Soon, she's grinding herself against my face, and I grip her ass, helping her balance.

"Anson!" She cries out as she comes against my mouth.

She moves her hand, covering her mouth as she screams my name, and I give her one last lick before I kiss my way up her body and seal her lips with mine.

"Bed. Now," I order, and she hurries to do as she's told.

She crawls onto the mattress, and I marvel at the sight of her curvy ass before me.

"So damn pretty," I tell her, and she blushes, spreading her legs in invitation.

I crawl onto the bed between her thighs, gripping my cock as I take her in. Her black hair is spread over my pillows, and she looks so perfect wrapped in my sheets.

"Are you ready for me, baby?" I ask her, and she nods enthusiastically.

I come down over her, bracing myself on one hand as I guide my cock to her snug opening.

We both sigh as I thrust home, and Lottie wastes no time wrapping her legs around my waist and her arms around my shoulders. I rock into her slowly, wanting to savor my second chance with her.

Her blue eyes meet mine, and I wonder how I ever missed it before. Her love for me is right there, shining in her pale blue eyes clear as day.

"I love you, Lottie. So much," I whisper, and she nods.

"I know. I love you too."

I claim her mouth then, keeping up the same slow pace as I slip my tongue into her mouth and kiss her. I try to pour all of my feelings into the kiss, into the way that I make love to her, and she just holds me tighter.

I'm so lucky to have found her. I wish I hadn't wasted so many years without telling her how I felt. I wish I hadn't listened to my dad's voice in my head or been afraid of losing Rhett or her these last few weeks.

I'm just glad that Lottie didn't give up on me.

We reach our peaks at the same time, and I stare into her eyes as we both come together. Our bodies lose tension at the same time, and her legs slowly drop from around my hips as I roll us and cradle her against my chest.

I can't stop kissing her forehead, smoothing her hair away from her face as we cuddle together.

"I'm not going anywhere," she promises me with a sleepy yawn, and I smile.

"Thank god for that," I whisper back, and she hugs me tighter as we both start to drift off to sleep.

THIRTEEN

Lottie

ONE YEAR LATER...

"DADDY SHOULD BE HOME ANY MINUTE," I coo to my daughter, and she smiles, trying to stick her foot in her mouth.

I smile down at her, passing her favorite stuffed animal over to her. She waves her arms when she sees the pink giraffe that Anson bought for her when she was first born. She immediately tries to put one of the feet into her mouth, and I laugh as I roll over, laying on my back next to her.

The front door opens, and I grin, turning my head to meet Anson's eyes.

"There's my girls," he says, tossing his hat onto the front table and dropping down onto his knees next to us.

He leans over, giving me a kiss before he reaches for our daughter, Honor.

Anson has been wrapped around Honor's little finger since she was born. As soon as he held her, I could see it on his face. He would do anything to keep her safe and make her happy.

"Rhett is coming over with pizza," Anson tells me, and I smile.

"Good. I didn't want to cook tonight. It's too hot out."

Anson laughs, and I take a moment to cherish this moment with our little family. Both Anson and Rhett got out of the SEALs after Rhett was shot. I don't know if it scared both of them or if it was because I was pregnant and they just wanted to be around more. Probably both, if I'm being honest.

They decided to get out, and they ended up starting their own security firm. They do some bodyguard work, though most of it is consultations for big companies who are looking to amp up their security.

Rhett and Anson seem to love their new career path and are thriving. The business has expanded so much already, and it's only been a few months. They're already talking about hiring more people in a few months, and I couldn't be prouder of both of them.

"Who wants pizza?" Rhett calls as he walks into the house.

Anson and I moved out of the apartment we all shared and bought a little house just outside the city. I love that there's less traffic out here, and it's a better place to raise a kid.

Rhett immediately hands the pizzas to me and reaches for Honor. He's the best uncle to her. He's so hands-on and patient. He loves spoiling her, and I know he would do anything to keep her safe too.

I set the pizza down in the kitchen and grab a few plates

for us. Honor just got done nursing not too long ago so she should be set for a little bit.

"You can put her in the high chair," I tell Rhett, and he looks at me like I'm crazy.

"I haven't seen my Honor all day, and you want me to just sit her in a high chair?"

"Right, my mistake," I say with a laugh, and he grins as he takes a seat with Honor in his lap.

Anson had been shocked when we learned it was a girl, and I had suggested the name Honor. He had started apologizing for disappearing for three weeks all over again, and I promised him that we were past that but that I just loved the name.

Truthfully, I loved how it reminded me of how we started. I had long since forgiven him for ghosting me. If the roles had been reversed, I probably would have done the same thing. It was rough for him to be in that position, and I know he was just scared of losing the only family he had ever known.

"Pepperoni?" Anson asks Rhett, and he nods distractedly.

Anson rolls his eyes at Rhett cooing at our daughter, and I just grin.

I grab a slice of pizza and join my brother and husband at the table. Honor is happy, chewing away on a rubber strawberry, and I smile as Anson squeezes my leg under the table.

We got married in a small ceremony at City Hall right after we officially got together. Anson said he was tired of wasting time, that he knew that we were meant to be together when he was fifteen and that had never changed or wavered in one day since.

When he proposed, I happily said yes, and we were

married within the week. We stuck around for a few months, making sure that Rhett was all better before we started looking for one of our own.

"How was your Valentine's Day date?" Rhett asks.

"It was... great," I say, sharing a secret smile with Anson.

It really was. This was the first time we had gone out since we had Honor. Rhett was nice enough to babysit for us, and we went down to the beach. We got tacos from that little taco truck that has the best Mexican food in town, and we just hung out. We talked and laughed and watched the sun go down. It was truly magical.

Anson and I may have also fooled around in his truck in a secret spot just down the road as well. It was a tight fit, but Anson made it work. He fucked me to two orgasms before we got dressed and came back home.

Best date ever.

Rhett pretends to gag, causing Honor to giggle, and I just smile, leaning over to kiss my husband.

"Love you, Lottie."

"That's good because I love you too."

"Gross. I'm so sorry that you had to see that, Honor," Rhett says, and she just giggles.

I join in, relaxing back in my chair as I enjoy this time with my family.

Want more Anson and Lottie? Then check out this bonus scene!

Looking for Rhett's story? Check it out here!

**Are you curious about Goldie and Boss Man?
How about Theo? Then check out the
Billionaire Bosshole series today!**